BLUEY

HOORAY, IT'S CHRISTMAS!
A STICKER & ACTIVITY BOOK

THIS STICKER & ACTIVITY BOOK BELONGS TO

~~Santa~~ ~~Elf~~

....

DECORATE THIS PAGE WITH STICKERS

PENGUIN YOUNG READERS LICENSES
An imprint of Penguin Random House LLC, New York

First published in Australia by Puffin Books, 2020

First published in the United States of America by Penguin Young Readers Licenses, an imprint of P

This book is based on the TV series *Bluey*.

Visit us online at penguinrandomhouse.com.

Manufactured in China

ISBN 9780593384176

D1314188

10 9 8 7 6 5 4 3 2 1 HH

BINGO'S
CHRISTMAS BINGO

Hooray, it's almost Christmas! Bluey and Bingo have planned something different for every day in December. Add a sticker when you complete an activity.

1

Visit the beach

2

Read Christmas books

3

Make Christmas cards

4

Write a letter to Veranda Santa

5

Play a game of Keepy Uppy

6

Make some
Christmas decorations

7

Video chat with
someone you love

8

Make your own wrapping paper
and wrap some presents

9

Decorate the tree

10

Dress up Bob Bilby as an elf

11

Make some custard

12 Put on a Christmas show

13 Play a game of charades

14 Make a Santa hat or some antlers

15 Treat yourself to dinner at a Fancy Restaurant

16 Visit your local Christmas market

17 Play a game of backyard cricket

18 Check out the local Christmas lights

19 Organize a family games night

20 Go for a swim, don't forget the sunscreen!

21 Hang your Santa stockings

22 Go on a Christmas treasure hunt

23 Throw something on the BBQ

24 Play Veranda Santa

25 Celebrate Christmas!

BANDIT'S
CHRISTMAS JOKES

Which one of Santa's reindeer has the best moves?

Dancer!

What do reindeer hang on their Christmas trees?

Horn-aments!

What do you get if you cross Santa with a detective?

Santa Clues

What is the name of Santa's most impolite reindeer?

Rude-olph!

What do you call Santa when he stops moving?

Santa Pause

CONNECT THE DOTS

What's that on Bluey's head?
Connect the dots to find out,
then color in the picture.

CHRISTMAS EVE STICKER SCENE

It's Christmas Eve in the Heeler house, and everyone is relaxing after a big dinner! Actually, wait . . . where is everyone? Can you complete the scene to find them?

COLOR THE PRESENTS

It's time to wrap some presents. Color in the patterns so they are ready to put under the tree!

SANTA SEARCH

Santa has a lot to do at Christmastime.
Can you help him find the words below?

BINGO   BLUEY   CHRISTMAS

DAD   ELF   MUFFIN   MUM

PRESENT   SANTA   SOCKS

W J P M G M I S U A
C C E U W O H H S N
V H H F Z E T M O G
B I R F B S L A C P
L O L I F I R F K R
U A B N S Y N J S E
E H L D A T B G L S
Y D A D N W M I O E
P R Y N T E R A Z N
A R Q V A U K D S T

CRAFTY CHRISTMAS LABELS

You will need:

- ☐ 8½" × 11" piece of paper or cardboard
- ☐ Scissors
- ☐ Hole puncher
- ☐ String or ribbon
- ☐ Stickers
- ☐ Pens or pencils

1 Fold your paper in half three times.

2 Unfold the paper and cut along the creases. You should now have eight labels!

3 Use a hole puncher to add a hole at the top of each label, then thread through a piece of string or ribbon.

4 Decorate one side of the label with stickers, or use your pens and pencils to draw some Christmas patterns!

Make sure to ask a grown-up to help with the cutting.

5 On the other side of the label, write your Christmas message.

Dear Bluey...

SANTA HAT HUNT

Bluey, Bingo, and Muffin are ready to play Veranda Santa, but they can't find the Santa hat. Help them through the maze so the games can begin!

FAMILY CHRISTMAS ALBUM

Find the matching stickers to complete the Heeler Family Christmas Album.

SO RELAXING.

RUUUFF!

WACKADOO!

I'M THE FLAMINGO QUEEN.

CHRISTMAS DELIVERIES

Veranda Santa needs to deliver the presents before Christmas Day. Can you help find the stickers that match each object on the paw-print path?

CREATE YOUR OWN SANTA HAT

You will need:
- ☐ Paper plate
- ☐ Red paint
- ☐ Paintbrush
- ☐ Scissors
- ☐ Glue
- ☐ Cotton balls

Make sure to ask a grown-up to help with the cutting.

1 Paint one side of the paper plate red. Let the paint dry.

2 Cut the paper plate in half. One plate will make two hats.

3 Curl one half of the paper plate into a cone shape and use glue to secure the two sides.

4 Glue a cotton ball to the top of the hat.

5 Tear cotton balls into strips and glue them all the way around the base of the hat.

Important
Let the glue dry before putting the hat on your head!

CONNECT THE DOTS

Who's wearing the Christmas headband?
Connect the dots to find out.

SNOW GLOBE SCENE

Here's your very own snow globe!
Draw whatever you like in the space below
and add feather stickers to the page.

VERANDA SANTA LETTER

Write a letter to Veranda Santa.
Make sure to send it before Christmas Eve!

Dear Veranda Santa,

My name is .... and I am .... years old.

I live in the great city of ....

This year I was:

☐ Very Good

☐ Quite Good

☐ A Little Bit Naughty

For Christmas, I would really like:

1. ....

2. ....

3. ....

On Christmas Eve, I promise to leave out

.... for you.

Merry Christmas!

Love, ...

CHRISTMAS
TREASURE HUNT

Christmas is about spending time with family.
Can you find these things around your home?
Add a feather sticker each time
you find something on the list!

SOMETHING MADE FROM TREES

PENCIL CASE

SOMETHING THAT GROWS

SOMETHING SOFT

ROLL OF TOILET PAPER

REMOTE CONTROL

SOMETHING OLD

SOMETHING RED OR GREEN

STICKER JIGSAW

It's time for an adventure! Find the missing puzzle pieces to complete the scene.

CUSTARD COOK-OFF!

Custard goes with everything. It's even nice on its own. Enjoy it warm, straight from the stove, or chill it in the fridge and have it cold!

serves 4

INGREDIENTS

- [ ] 2 eggs
- [ ] 3 tablespoons of cornstarch
- [ ] 3 cups of whole milk
- [ ] 3 tablespoons of powdered sugar
- [ ] 1 teaspoon of vanilla extract

DIRECTIONS

1. Whisk eggs, cornstarch, and milk together in a saucepan over medium-low heat until smooth.

2. Continue whisking the mixture on the stove until custard becomes thick and creamy.

3. Remove from the heat, then whisk in sugar and vanilla.

Ask a grown-up to help!

HINT

Bring the eggs to room temperature before cooking.

Do not add sugar while on the heat as the custard will stick to the pan.

GAME MATCHUP

Are you ready to play?
Find the sticker that goes with each game!

SPOT THE DIFFERENCE

There are ten differences between these two pictures of the Heeler house. Can you find them all?

ANSWERS

HIDE-AND-SEEK

Bluey and Bingo can't wait to find the presents Veranda Santa has hidden in their room. Can you help them search for all ten?

FEATHER FUN

Everyone has surprised Bandit with a pillow fight! Finish coloring in the picture and count how many feathers there are.

Answer: 14

CHRISTMAS PATTERNS

Bluey loves a challenge. Can you help her to complete the patterns below by finding the correct sticker to go next?

DECORATE THE TREE

Wow! Look at this amazing Christmas tree.
Can you use the stickers to decorate it? What will go on top?

The fun never stops! Can you spot Surfing Santa in every activity? Long Dog is also hidden somewhere in the book!

Answer: Long Dog is on page 21.